Double Act

PLAY EDITION

www.kidsatrandomhouse.co.uk

Double Act

PLAY EDITION

Dramatized for the stage
by Vicky Ireland
from the novel
by Jacqueline Wilson

Corgi Yearling Books

DOUBLE ACT (PLAY SCRIPT)
A CORGI YEARLING BOOK 0 440 86631 6

Published in Great Britain by Corgi Yearling,
an imprint of Random House Children's Books

This edition published 2004

3 5 7 9 10 8 6 4 2

Original text copyright © Jacqueline Wilson, 1995
Play script copyright © Vicky Ireland, 2004

The right of Vicky Ireland to be identified as the author
of this work has been asserted in accordance with the
Copyright, Designs and Patents Act 1988.

Papers used by Random House Children's Books are natural,
recyclable products made from wood grown in sustainable forests.
The manufacturing processes conform to the environmental
regulations of the country of origin.

Typeset in Century Schoolbook by
Palimpsest Book Production Limited, Polmont, Stirlingshire

Corgi Yearling Books are published by
Random House Children's Books,
61–63 Uxbridge Road, London W5 5SA,
a division of The Random House Group Ltd,
in Australia by Random House Australia (Pty) Ltd,
20 Alfred Street, Milsons Point, Sydney, NSW 2061, Australia,
in New Zealand by Random House New Zealand Ltd,
18 Poland Road, Glenfield, Auckland 10, New Zealand,
and in South Africa by Random House (Pty) Ltd,
Endulini, 5A Jubilee Road, Parktown 2193, South Africa

THE RANDOM HOUSE GROUP Limited Reg. No. 954009
www.kidsatrandomhouse.co.uk

A CIP catalogue record for this book is available from the British
Library.

Printed and bound in Great Britain by
Cox & Wyman Ltd, Berkshire, Reading

Double Act was first performed at the Polka Theatre from 30 January to 12 April 2003, then toured by Watershed Productions throughout the UK.

The original cast was:

RUBY BARKER — Helen Rutter

GARNET BARKER — Catherine Kinsella

RICHARD BARKER/BRIAN 'FERRET FACE' JONES/AUDITION TWINS' MUM — John McCraw

ROSE/JUDY/WARREN/CASTING AGENT — Laura Sheppard

GRAN (MRS DUNBAR)/MISS DEBENHAM/JASON/AUDITION TWINS' MUM — Bonny Ambrose

JEREMY 'THE BLOB' THREADGOLD/MR LEWIS/MR BAINES/ CASTING ASSISTANT/GUARDIAN ADVERTISEMENT/POSTMAN — Ben Redfern

All other parts played by members of the cast.

DIRECTOR — Vicky Ireland

DESIGNER — Gemma Fripp

CHOREOGRAPHER — Ian Waller

LIGHTING DESIGN — Jim Simmons

SOUND AND ORIGINAL MUSIC — Steven Markwick

CHARACTERS

RUBY BARKER

The elder twin by twenty minutes. She feels this makes her the boss. She's definitely bossy – a fiery, funny, ultra-determined girl who is desperate to be an actress.

GARNET BARKER

The younger twin. She nearly always does what Ruby says. She's sweet, shy and living in Ruby's shadow.

RICHARD BARKER

Their dad. Bookish, kind, fun. Out of his depth as a single parent with lively twins whom he adores. Deliriously in love with Rose and desperate to start a new life.

ROSE

Dad's girlfriend. Warm, mother-earth figure; fun, patient, very tolerant but not stupid; very much her own person.

GRAN

Strict and prickly, her patience limited because of painful arthritis. Finds new lease of life with Mr Lewis.

ALBERT LEWIS

Gran's elderly neighbour in the sheltered flat.

JEREMY 'THE BLOB' THREADGOLD

Leader of gang. Typical bullyboy in group, but shows respect for Ruby's courage when on his own, and proves good fun and likeable.

BRIAN 'FERRET-FACE' JARVIS	*Jeremy's side-kick.*
WARREN	*Member of gang.*
JASON	*Member of gang.*
MISS DEBENHAM	*Village school teacher, pleasant and normal.*
MR BAINES	*Village taxi and video hire man.*
JUDY	*A pupil.*
MISS LAVENHAM	*Villager.*
TICKET INSPECTOR	
MUM 1	
MUM 2	
CASTING AGENT	
CASTING ASSISTANT	
TV PRESENTER	
POSTMAN	
TEACHER	

The play can be performed with a minimum cast of six, or up to thirty with no doubling and using extra cast in village, school, gang and London scenes.

SETTINGS

ACT ONE: The twins' home: living and eating area, Gran's chair, lampstand/Gran's flat/In the car/The countryside/ The Red Bookshop: living and eating area/The riverbank/The classroom/The playground

ACT TWO: The video shop/The streets of London/Inside a theatre/Sitting exams in school

DESIGN

We thought it was important to base design ideas on the book's illustrations and the whole idea of books and paper. The set was made to resemble a huge sheet of paper, bordered by piles of books. It had one door. We used six chairs and one table plus an armchair and lampstand for Gran. We also made props out of paper – i.e. cut-out pictures to put the face through, cut-out twin dolls for the auditionees, bits of the story coming out of a pop-up book, etc. Branches were added to the piles of books to make the countryside.

STYLE AND MUSIC

Movement and dance were important as alternative methods of telling the story, backed up by modern music.

ACT ONE

The twins' home.
> (*Music. Enter* RUBY *and* GARNET *from opposite sides. They are dressed the same and both have their hair in plaits. They do a short, fun 'twin' dance sequence: they dance the same steps and mirror each other's actions.*)

RUBY (*to audience*): We're twins. I'm Ruby. She's Garnet. Not many people can tell us apart. Well, until we start talking. I tend to go on and on; Garnet is much quieter.

GARNET: That's because I can't get a word in edgeways.

RUBY: I eat a bit more than her but I don't get fatter because I charge around more. I hate sitting still. I'm the oldest by twenty minutes – the bossy baby who pushed out first.

> (*They laugh and fight.* GRAN *enters. She*

walks with difficulty because of her arthritis.)

GRAN: Girls, girls! Where is your dad? He should have been back ages ago. I've had the dinner turned down low for the last half-hour and my Yorkshire's gone all sad and soggy.

RUBY: Yorkshire pud – yummy yummy in my tummy.

GRAN: Yes, well, I just hope he hurries up. (*Exits.*)

GARNET: Dad *is* all right, isn't he?

RUBY: Of course he is. He's only been at a car boot sale, for heaven's sake. I expect he's bought piles of books and he's having trouble stuffing them all in the car. You know what he's like. Books, books, books, that's all he ever thinks about. We can hardly move in this house for books.

GARNET: Yes, but he's not usually this late. And he likes Gran's Sunday lunch as much as we do. What if he's had an accident?

RUBY: Oh, Garnet, you're such a worry-guts. (*To audience*) That was our gran, by the way, just then. We live with her and our dad. She used to work in this posh fashion house, pinning and sewing all day long.

(*They demonstrate.*) Then, after— (*They stop.*) Well, Gran had to look after us, so she did dressmaking at home. But now her arthritis is so bad, she can't sew any more. It makes all your joints go stiff (*They demonstrate*) and her fingers won't work. So, there we are. That's us. Dad, Gran, Garnet and me. I have to say, everything's a bit boring at the moment, but maybe soon we'll get our big chance and achieve our lifetime's ambition and become famous actresses.

(*Music in. Cut-out picture of famous actress comes on.* RUBY *puts face through. Then picture exits. Music out.*)

GARNET: I don't want to be an actress.

RUBY: Of course you do. Honestly, Garnet, stop spoiling it. (*To audience*) She can be a bit shy at times. She doesn't think we'll make it as film stars, but I keep telling her all we need is *confidence!* (*To* GARNET) Well, if that's not what you wanted to say, say something yourself.

GARNET (*to audience*): I'm not used to talking about me. It's always *us*. I *do* like writing though. I like making up plays and I don't mind acting them out when it's just Ruby and me, but I can't bear proper acting. We were twin sheep in the nativity play when we were still in the Infants, and it was one of the most awful experiences of my life. Not the *most* awful, of course. That was when—

RUBY: Look, you're not telling any of that sad stuff – I won't let you. You can't reject Fame just because of one unfortunate experience being a sheep when we were little. (*To audience*) She got so worked up and nervous when we had to perform . . . here we come (*opens pop-up book nativity play*), me and Garnet (*indicates twin sheep*) . . . that she peed on stage! But it didn't really matter. I mean, that's what real sheep do all the time. They go all over the place. Baa, piss, baa, piss . . . Everyone thought it was ever so funny. Except Garnet.

GARNET: You mean pig! (*Closes book.*)

RUBY: You were the one who mentioned it first. Oh, stop fussing!

    (DAD *enters with large box of books. He takes off hat and scarf.* ROSE *follows.*)

DAD: Hello, I'm home.

    (DAD *and* ROSE *move downstage.*)

RUBY: Dad! Thank goodness – now we can eat. I'm starving.

    (GRAN *enters.*)

4

DAD: Hi, everyone. Sorry we're late. Oh, this is Rose. Rose, this is Gran and these are the twins.

ROSE: Hello, Gran . . . twins.

GRAN: Hello, Rose.

TWINS (*mumble*): Hello.

DAD: Rose helped me with the books, then her car wouldn't start, so I gave her a lift and we popped into the pub for a drink, and rather than just have a sandwich I asked her back for lunch—

ROSE: Which is such a treat for me – it's ages since I had a proper Sunday dinner.

DAD: So, here we are. But first, books . . .

GRAN: Oh, not *more* books. The floorboards won't stand the weight. (*Sits in armchair.*)

DAD: Gran, these are for you. You can sit in your chair with your feet up, a box of Milk Tray and a pile of juicy love stories.

GRAN: Thank you, Richard. Very kind.

DAD: Well, they were a bargain. Couldn't resist them. Now, some for Garnet. Here we are. (*Hands her some books.*)

GARNET: Let's see – *Little Women, What Katy Did, The Twins at St Clare's*, book one – great! Thanks, Dad.

DAD: And Ruby.

RUBY: *My Life in the Spotlight: the true story of famous actress Greta Green.* This will be very useful research for when we become famous actresses.

DAD: And for me, Boswell, Thackeray and Hardy. All nice editions too.

GRAN: My, you have been busy.

(*Pause. It all goes quiet.*)

DAD: Well, I'm glad you like them. There's not a problem, is there, Gran?

GRAN: No, of course not. There's plenty of food. I'm afraid the beef will be a bit overdone and I can't take pride in my Yorkshire today. It was lovely and light and fluffy, but—

ROSE: But I waylaid your son-in-law and kept him down the pub and mucked up your meal. Sorry. (*Laughs.*)

DAD: Can I help?

GRAN: No thank you, Richard, you'll just get under my feet. The twins will do it. Come on, girls – table, please.

(*Music in.* TWINS *carry in table, in time to music, then exit. Others assemble five chairs and sit.* TWINS *re-enter with tray of pop-up food laid flat except for one large dish of meat and veg.* GRAN *pretends to dole out food to each plate. As she does so, the recipient flicks up food with their knife. When meal is served, Gran's serving-dish food is laid flat. The meal is also eaten in time to music, with conversation and enjoyment. As music fades they push their food flat.*)

ROSE: Must be fascinating being a twin. I think I'm beginning to spot the difference. Now, you're Ruby, right, and you're Garnet?

TWINS: Yes. Right.

DAD: Wrong. *That's* Ruby and *that's* Garnet. They're a pair of jokers. Even Gran and I get confused at times.

GRAN: Speak for yourself. I'm sorry the beef was so dry. It was done to a turn an hour or so back. Anyway. Apple pie and cream? Help me clear the plates, girls.

(TWINS *clear plates, then exit.*)

DAD: Gran's got them well trained.

GRAN: They're very good girls.

DAD: They don't take a blind bit of notice of me though.

(*Music in. As before,* TWINS *enter in time.* RUBY *carries tray and they unload pudding dishes. This time the apple pie on each plate is already upright. They all eat in time and, as music fades, they push their apple pie flat.*)

ROSE: Hmm, that was really delicious . . . Do you know, I think I really can tell you

apart now. You're Ruby and you're Garnet.
Yes? Right?

DAD: Well . . . not *quite* right. Stop teasing
poor Rose. I'm afraid they've swapped
seats. They're always doing it. I'd just call
each one 'Twin' and be done with it.

ROSE: Oh, I think that's awful. I couldn't
stand that if I was a twin. You're two
separate people who just happen to be
sisters, aren't you, Garnet and Ruby? Or
Ruby and Garnet. Whichever. I'm really
muddled now.

RUBY: We like being called 'Twin'.

GARNET: That's what they call us at school.

RUBY: We are twins . . .

GARNET: . . . so we like . . .

RUBY: . . . being called . . .

TWINS: . . . twins.

ROSE: Right, OK. Got it. (*Pause.*) Delicious
apple pie, Mrs Dunbar.

GRAN: Thank you.

DAD: Yes, Gran's a smashing cook, especially
when it comes to good old Sunday lunch.
And her bread and butter pudding is even
better than her apple pie, isn't it, twins?
You must try it sometime.

ROSE: I'd love to.

DAD: Good. How about next Sunday?
(*Music in.* DAD *and* TWINS *clear table*

and chairs. GRAN *sits in armchair.* DAD
sees ROSE *to door and they exchange a*
clumsy kiss. ROSE *exits.* DAD *turns with*
an expectant glow.)

DAD: Bye, Rose . . . Well, what do you think
of her?

(TWINS *mime being sick, then laugh.*)

DAD: All right, all right. You've done enough
clowning around for one day.

GRAN: Yes, don't be so rude, you two.

DAD: Did you like Rose, Gran?

GRAN: Well. She seems nice enough. I
suppose. A bit . . . pushy, inviting herself
to lunch like that.

DAD: No, I invited her. I didn't think you'd
make such a big deal about it, actually.
You've always said you wished I'd socialize
a bit more, bring a few friends home, not
stay wrapped up in the past.

GRAN: Yes, dear. And I mean it. I'm only too
pleased that you want to bring people
back. Though if you could have just
phoned to give me a bit of warning . . .
And you do want to go carefully with that
type of woman—

DAD (*getting agitated*): What do you mean,
type?

GRAN: Now, now, Richard, don't get yourself
in such a silly state. It's just that she

seems so eager. She's never set eyes on you before today and yet she's all over you, even trying to act like one of the family.

DAD: I've known Rose for months, if you must know. She's got her own bric-a-brac stall in the arcade – we're forever bumping into each other at boot fairs. I've always wanted to get to know her better – she's so bubbly and warm and friendly. I don't know how you can talk about her like that – she's a lovely girl.

GRAN: Girl! She'll never see thirty again.

DAD (*shouts*): Well, neither will I. So it's about time I started making the most of my life, OK? And if that means seeing Rose, then that's what I'll do. (*Exits.*)

GRAN: Help me up, girls, I'm stuck. (TWINS *help to heave* GRAN *out of armchair*.) I'm going to have a little lie down. Be good girls, now. (GRAN *takes books from* GARNET.) Oh, thank you very much. (GRAN *exits.*)

GARNET: Dad really likes Rose, doesn't he? I've never seen him like that before. All moony.

RUBY: Forget about Dad. Let's get on with telling about us. Go on.

GARNET: I don't want to go on. I want to

stop. No, I want to go backwards. Back past today, back past the 'ordinary us-twins-and-Dad-and-Gran-day-after-day' part. Back through the awful bit when Mum died and—

RUBY: Stop it, stop it, stop it!

GARNET: No, Ruby. We can't stop now. We've got to remember, don't you see? We've got to make Dad remember, and then he'll stop seeing Rose.

RUBY: Oh. All right. But tell it quickly. The bit about Mum. Tell it as if it were a story and not real so it won't hurt so much.

GARNET: Once upon a time (*Music in.* GARNET *puts on Dad's hat.*) a man called Richard fell in love with a girl called Opal. (GARNET *puts scarf around* RUBY'*s neck.*) They got their own flat. They got married. They had twin daughters . . . and though they grew, they still had cuddles with Mum; she made them feel so safe . . . The twins started school. Opal and Richard went to work and at the weekends they did fun things. But then Opal got sick. She lay on the sofa at home. Richard stopped working to look after her. But she couldn't get better. She got worse and worse and, in the end, she died. There – I've said it. (*Music ends.*)

Gran lives with us now but she's not like a mother. No one can be like a mother to us ever again. We're a new family now, with just Dad and Gran—

RUBY: And we don't ever have rows in our family. It's all Rose's fault.

GARNET: Yes. It's all Rose's fault. (*Shouts*) Stupid, frizzy, dizzy Rose!

(*Music in.* DAD *enters carrying book. He has smart new shirt and trousers on. He puts book on floor then turns to* TWINS *for approval. They look appalled. He goes to door.* ROSE *enters.* TWINS *watch, disgusted, and exit.* ROSE *and* DAD *embrace and slow dance.* GRAN *enters with washing basket. Music fades.*)

DAD: I've got something for you. (*Gives* ROSE *book.*)

ROSE: Oh, wow! I've been looking for this for ages.

DAD: Told you I'd find it.

ROSE: Oh, I love it. Thank you.

DAD: You're welcome.

ROSE: And I've got something for you.

DAD: Oh, what is it, Rose? (TWINS *enter as* DAD *receives Mickey Mouse tie.*) Where did you find this?

ROSE: Try it on. My friend sells them – it

wasn't expensive. I just saw it and thought of you . . . There, you look really cute, Ricky.

(DAD *turns to show* TWINS.)

RUBY (*to audience*): Ricky! It doesn't half make you feel sicky.

GRAN: His name's Richard. We've always called him Richard. No one ever calls him Ricky.

ROSE: *I* call him Ricky. (GRAN *sucks in breath*.) Oh dear, is the pain really bad?

GRAN: No, I'm fine, thank you. (*Exits*.)

RUBY (*to audience*): You're the one that's the pain.

DAD: So, I'll pick you up at seven, OK?

ROSE: You bet. See you later, girls. Bye, sweetie. (*Exits*.)

DAD: Bye, gorgeous. (DAD *shuts door.* TWINS *start to leave*.) No, wait a minute. Sit down, you two. There's something I want to talk to you about. It's serious. It's about Gran. (TWINS *sit either side of chair*.) She's a very proud woman, your gran, and she wouldn't like to admit it, but she's very poorly. Her arthritis is really bad – she's in a lot of pain. Some mornings she can't even get out of bed, let alone down the stairs. In fact it's got to the point where she can't manage at all without proper

13

help. I— we can't afford round-the-clock care, so I've been to see about sheltered housing for her.

RUBY: She's going to live in a bus shelter?! (*Music in. Cut-out picture of Gran in bus shelter comes on.* GRAN *puts face through. Music out.*)

DAD: No, no, nothing like that. (*Music in.* DAD *chases picture off. Music out.*) It's a special place where elderly people live, where they're safe and can be looked after. She'll have a little flat on the ground floor with a home help to visit every day and an alarm button, in case of emergencies.

RUBY: But that's terrible.

DAD: I'm sorry, girls, we really have no choice—

GARNET: But Dad, we don't want her to go. (GRAN *enters.*)

GRAN: Don't want who to go?

DAD: Um, I've just been telling the girls about your smashing new flat—

GRAN: Oh, have you?

RUBY: And we think it's a terrible idea.

GRAN: Well, I don't think I've much choice. Your dad says he can't afford any extra help and I don't want to be any more of a burden than I already am. (*Starts to go.*)

DAD: Hang on, Gran, don't go. There's something else I need to discuss . . .

GRAN: So, what is it? (*Sits.*)

DAD: Well, I've lost my job. To be exact, I've been made redundant – but to be absolutely honest I don't really care. I've always hated that boring old office . . .

GRAN: So how are you going to manage without your boring old salary? Oh, Richard, you're such a fool. How could you spoil your chances like that? And you've got the twins to think of too—

DAD: It wasn't my fault.

GRAN: You've never shown the right attitude. And since you've taken up with that Rose, you've turned into . . . into a hippy!

DAD: Oh, for goodness' sake—

GRAN: All those silly shirts and ties. Of course they got rid of you. You look ridiculous. So what are you going to do now? Have you looked at Jobs Vacant in the papers?

DAD: I don't want that sort of job any more. I've been thinking. They're giving me quite a bit of cash as my redundancy pay. It's my chance for a whole new start. We could sell up here, get a little shop in the country somewhere. A bookshop. You've always been on and on at me to sell some of my books. Now's my chance!

GRAN: You're talking nonsense. Well, I've got my new flat to look forward to so you can count me out.

RUBY: And us. We don't want to move to a silly shop in the country.

DAD: But it'll be fun—

GRAN: And what about Rose? She won't like being left behind.

DAD: Well, Rose is coming with us.

RUBY: What!

(TWINS *sit together.*)

DAD: I've already discussed it with her. She's really keen.

RUBY: Oh no! (DAD *and* GRAN *continue talking during the next few lines.*) We don't want to live with her. (*Music in. Cut-out picture of Rose comes on with* ROSE's *face through.*) We wish she'd get greenfly—

GARNET: And mildew—

RUBY: And wilt!

BOTH: Ha!

(*Picture exits. Music out.*)

DAD: Good. So, it's all decided and settled. Great! (*Exits.*)

RUBY (*shouting*): No, it is not all decided and settled! Stupid countryside! Stupid Rose.

What's going on, Garnet? This is awful!
(*Stamps around.*)

GRAN: Now, now. Behave yourself. You can if
you try. You're going to have to remember
everything I've taught you when you go to
live in the country. Rose isn't the type to
bother with good manners.

RUBY: But Gran, I don't want to go! I don't
want to leave you. (*Sits on* GRAN's *lap.*)

GRAN: Ow! Watch my hip! And my knee!
Ruby, you great lump, get off me!

GARNET: Can I have a cuddle too? (*Sits on*
GRAN's *other side and starts to cry.*)

RUBY: Stop it, Garnet.

GRAN: Dear, oh dear. (*Sniffs.*) We'd better
turn off the waterworks. I don't want a
puddle in my chair.

RUBY: Oh Gran, please please please come
with us.

GRAN: Now don't you start, young Ruby. You
heard your dad. It's all settled and
decided. I've got my new flat and that's
where I'm going.

GARNET: But we'll miss you so, Gran!

GRAN: And I'll miss both of you, my girls. But
you can come and stay with me – you can
sleep either end of the sofa and bring your
sleeping bags – and maybe I'll come to
your new place for Christmas.

GARNET: Not maybe. You've got to come.

GRAN: We'll see. There's probably no point. Rose doesn't have a clue about cooking. She probably won't even bother to have a proper turkey.

RUBY: So why can't we all come to you for Christmas, Gran, and then we can have Christmas dinner the way you do it, with cranberry sauce and chipolatas and chestnut stuffing!

GRAN: That oven in my new flat is so small you'd have problems cooking a chicken in it. Sorry, pet. No more Christmas dinners.

GARNET: No more roast potatoes with special crispy bits and Christmas pud with little silver charms and traffic-light jelly – red, yellow, green—

GRAN: I think you're going to miss my cooking more than you'll miss me. Come on now, you're squashing me something chronic. Anyway, we can't sit around here gossiping. Got to get ready for my move . . . Help me up. (TWINS *help* GRAN *to her feet.*)

(*Music in. Passage of time.* ROSE *enters with large cardboard box.* GRAN *exits.* DAD *enters with another box, then* TWINS *bring on more boxes, which are stacked.*)

DAD *and* ROSE *exit, leaving* TWINS *staring at pile. Music fades as* DAD *rushes in with letter.*)

DAD: Listen, you two, Guess what! I've bought a shop.

TWINS: What!

DAD: This sweet old couple are retiring and are happy to move out straight away. Your gran's got her sheltered flat. Rose only rents her room, so she hasn't got any problems. It's perfect!

RUBY: You've gone and bought a shop. Without even asking us to see if we liked it. But that's not fair.

DAD: Don't worry, you'll love it – I promise. The village is right out in the country, beside a river, with hills all around. There's just this one street of shops. Ours is in the middle. We'll fit it out with shelves for the books and Rose can have the window for her bric-a-brac. And there's plenty of room upstairs. You two can have the attic bedroom – you'll like that. Just got to get Gran settled and then we're off. Come on.

(*Music in. Gran's armchair, lampstand and boxes moved upstage to create Gran's flat. The family's suitcases brought on downstage.* GRAN *enters with coat and hat on.* DAD *and* TWINS *join* GRAN *and move upstage – signifying Gran's flat. Music fades.*)

DAD: Here we are then. It's quite a nice little flat, isn't it? Really snug, with just enough room. What do you think?

GARNET: Oh, Gran, please don't look so sad.

RUBY: It doesn't look like a home. Not Gran's home anyway.

DAD: See, here's your chair and all your bits. It's on the ground floor so there's no stairs to bother with, and you'll have someone to help every day. (MR LEWIS *enters with a bunch of flowers.*) It'll be so much better than struggling at home, won't it?

MR LEWIS: Excuse me. Hope I'm not interrupting. The name's Lewis, Albert Lewis. I live next door. So you're the new girl, eh? Just popped in to say hello and welcome you with these. (*Gives* GRAN *flowers.*) Grew them myself.

GRAN: Thank you. They're lovely – that's very kind of you, Mr Lewis.

MR LEWIS: Don't mention it. Your family, eh? How do? Well, I hope you settle in all right. They're not too bad, these flats, once you get used to them. And if I can be of any help, you just let me know. Bye for now.

DAD: Thank you, Mr Lewis.

ALL: Bye.

(MR LEWIS *exits*.)

DAD: You'd better watch it, Gran – gone and got yourself a boyfriend already! (GRAN *doesn't smile. Awkward pause*.) Anyway, I hope you'll be really happy here. I'm sure it's for the best. You'll be well looked after and things won't be so difficult. We'll see you very soon. Bye for now. (DAD *kisses* GRAN *and exits*.)

GRAN: You won't forget me, will you?

(*Music in. Emotional hugs goodbye with* TWINS.)

RUBY: Never.

GARNET: Oh, Gran. We're going to miss you so much.

RUBY: So much.

(GRAN *turns and exits upstage.* TWINS *move downstage*.)

RUBY (*to audience*): And our friends.

GARNET: And our school.

RUBY: And our home.

TWINS: Everything.

(*Music changes.* TWINS *bring on four chairs and make car.* DAD *and* ROSE *collect suitcases from downstage and put in boot. They all get in car. Music fades as car sound effects start. Mimed journey.*)

ROSE (*reading map*): We must remember to take junction twenty-one.

DAD: Give me a shout when it's coming up. (TWINS *sneeze loudly.*)

DAD: I thought we could pop into the other shops on the high street once we've settled in – let them know we've arrived. (TWINS *cough loudly, pause then laugh loudly.*) Pack it in.

TWINS: Pack it in what, Dad?

DAD: Less of the cheek.

ROSE: How do they do that?

TWINS: How do we do what?

ROSE: Stop it! You're giving me the creeps. Can you really read each other's thoughts?

DAD: Of course they can't.

ROSE: Then how can they say the same thing at the same time in that weird way?

DAD: I don't know.

TWINS: We know. (*They start singing 'My Bonny Lies Over the Ocean' loudly with hand gestures.*)

DAD: Cut it out, twins. (TWINS *start playing scissors around Dad's head, cutting his hair.*) Oh, very funny. Not when I'm

driving. (TWINS *change to stabbing* ROSE.)
What are you playing at, you two?
(TWINS *shrug and make rude noises as*
DAD *hugs* ROSE. *Pause. Three tree
branches are added to the set to signify
that they have arrived in the country.*)

ROSE: Oh look – it's really pretty now.

DAD: Hmmm, this is more like it.

RUBY: Are we nearly there yet, Dad?

DAD: Not far now.

ROSE: Look at the cottages.

RUBY (*to* GARNET): Oh no, I feel a bit— (*She
is sick on* GARNET's *knee.*)

GARNET: Ugh, Ruby! What are you doing?

RUBY: Dad?

DAD: What?

RUBY: I'm gonna be— (*She is sick all over*
ROSE's *back.*)

DAD: Oh no! Ruby, are you all right? Rose,
have you got something to clean it up
with? We're nearly there now . . . Not
far now. Ahh, this is us . . . (*Stops the
car.*)

ROSE (*to* DAD): It's all right, I'll deal with it.
(*All get out. Country sounds – birds
singing.* DAD *unpacks the car.* ROSE *and*
TWINS *clean up with tissues.* ROSE *speaks
and* TWINS *answer in asides.*)

ROSE: Come on, you two. Look, I don't care if

you act like idiots, but it isn't half upsetting
your dad. (RUBY *smiles*.) Don't you want
your dad to be happy?

GARNET (*to audience*): Not with you.

ROSE: He's had a really tough time the last
few years. He nearly went to pieces after
your mum died—

RUBY (*to audience*): How *dare* she!

ROSE: But he kept going for your sake. He
did his best to get on with your gran,
though she can be so difficult at times.

GARNET: Fancy having the *nerve* to criticize
Gran . . .

ROSE: He didn't have any fun, he never went
out anywhere – he was so lonely.

RUBY: But he had *us*!

ROSE: He kept slaving away at that boring
old job in the city, though it nearly drove
him crazy. He was like an old man and
he's barely thirty.

    (DAD *dismantles car and takes suitcases
    through the door.*)

GARNET: She's mad. He *is* old. He's our dad.

ROSE: But now he's got this big chance. A
whole new life. Something that he's always
wanted. And he's been like a little kid – so
excited. But you two are spoiling it all.
Can't you see that? (*She moves upstage to
join* DAD.)

RUBY: Yes, we can see it. That's what we want.

GARNET: It's not us that's spoiling everything. She's got it all wrong.

BOTH: It's her. It's her it's her it's her. We hate her!! (*Move upstage to join* DAD *and* ROSE.)

DAD: And here we are, the village of Cussop. Isn't it sweet? And this is our new home. (*All turn upstage.*) Come on, let's get inside and take a look.

ROSE: Yes, come on, girls. Quickly.

DAD: Let's get the kettle on.

> (*Music in as they exit through door. Two villagers enter.*)

MRS LAVENHAM (*with dog*): Come along, Princess.

MR BAINES (*with dog*): Come on, Hendrix.

MRS LAVENHAM: Ah – morning, Baines.

MR BAINES: Morning, Mrs Lavenham.

MRS LAVENHAM: Baines, here a moment. (MR BAINES *joins her.*) Look, the shop's been sold.

MR BAINES: Oh, I knew it was up for sale, but I didn't know anyone had bought it.

MRS LAVENHAM: Have a look in the window. See what you can see.

MR BAINES: Will do. (*Peers through window.*) Nothing to report, Mrs Lavenham.

(*Music fades.* ROSE, DAD *and* TWINS *appear with bucket and sponges.*)

DAD: Morning.

VILLAGERS: Morning.

DAD: We've just moved in.

MR BAINES: Oh, lovely. Well, I hope you settle in all right. (*Exits.*)

MRS LAVENHAM: Welcome to Cussop. Good day to you all.

DAD: Thank you very much.

ROSE: Thank you.

MRS LAVENHAM (*to dog*): Come along, girl. (*Exits.*)

DAD: Listen, I've had this brilliant idea. I'm going to call it the Red Bookshop because of my three girls. Rubies are red, Garnets are red, and Roses are red. So let's go the whole hog and paint the front red too. What do you think?

ROSE: That's a great idea. We'll wash it down while you buy the paint.

DAD: Fantastic. Won't be long. (*Music in.* DAD *exits.*)

ROSE: Come on then, girls. (*Mimes washing the shop with sponge.*) Come on.

(TWINS *take a sponge each and join in reluctantly. Music fades and they throw their sponges in bucket.*)

RUBY: We're fed up with this lark.

(TWINS *saunter off*.)

ROSE: Hey, come back, you lazy beasts! (*Flicks water at them.* RUBY *picks up the bucket and chucks it at* ROSE.) Argh!! Oh, you two!

(ROSE *exits in disgust with bucket. Music in.* TWINS *laugh and dance into the country, using steps to show freedom and a journey, crossing a log bridge and going through undergrowth, etc.* GANG *enter from opposite side in time to music.* BLOB *stands and fishes over front of stage. The* GANG *sit around him.* GARNET *slips and her bottom gets covered in mud.* RUBY *laughs.* GARNET *tries to wipe off the mud and cries. Music fades.*)

RUBY: Why do you always have to be such a baby? Look, it's your own fault for falling over. It doesn't matter anyway – they're only your old jeans. And Rose can't tell us off because she's not our mother or any part of our family, so stop fussing.

GARNET: But I can't go back through the village like this. People will laugh at me.

RUBY: No they won't. They won't even notice, honest.

(TWINS *start to exit*.)

BLOB: By the way, Ferret, my mum says it's

all right for us to have the tent to camp in the graveyard tonight.

FERRET: Brilliant. My mum says I've got to be back by two though.

BLOB: Eh, well, you'll have run off by then anyway.

FERRET: No I won't, Jerry.

BLOB: Yeah, you will.

(FERRET *and* BLOB *turn, see* GARNET *and laugh at her.*)

BLOB: Hey, look at that one. She's covered in muck!

FERRET: Pooed yer pants, did you!

BLOB: Smells like it too.

(GANG *all laugh.* TWINS *turn and march up to them.*)

BLOB: Oh look, they're both the same—

RUBY: What's so funny?

TWINS: What's so funny?

BLOB: You are. Townies. You can't take mud.

RUBY: Being covered in mud is funny, is it?

TWINS: Funny, is it?

BLOB: Yeah. It is.

RUBY: Well, have a big laugh then.

(TWINS *throw mud at the* GANG *and run.*)

BLOB: Ooh, it's gone into me eyes! OK, gang, come on, let's go get 'em! (*Music in.* GANG *chase the* TWINS.) Where've they gone?

FERRET: Jerry, they're going down the cobbly
   path.
      (TWINS *enter upstage.*)
BLOB: Let's go and cut them off before they
   get there. Come on. Ah, we've missed
   them already. They must have gone the
   other side of the river. Come on, let's go
   over the monkey bridge. C'mon, Ferret.
      (GANG *exit.* TWINS *come out of hiding
      and move downstage. Music fades.*)
RUBY: Their faces! Oh, Garnet, that was
   wicked. Twin-grin!
GARNET: Twin-grin.
      (TWINS *pull faces.* GARNET *looks behind
      her nervously.*)
RUBY: Relax. They'll have gone back to their
   stupid fishing.
GARNET: Maybe. But they could still get us . . .
      (TWINS *sit at front of stage.*)
RUBY: Well, we'll get them straight back.
   Especially that blobby one.
GARNET: But they'll all start hating us then.
   And we've got to go to school with them,
   haven't we?
RUBY: We won't go to that stupid little school.
   We'll sneak off by ourselves.
GARNET: But they'll find out and we'll get
   into trouble. We're in pretty big trouble
   now. We can't go home because Rose'll get

29

us, and we can't go back that way because those kids'll get us.

RUBY: Garnet? (*Puts her arm round* GARNET *and cuddles her.*)

GARNET: You know what, I really miss Gran.

RUBY: I know. I do too, ever so much.

GARNET: She was strict and she got cross and sometimes she even used to smack us, but it never hurt 'cause of her poor old hands.

RUBY: She was only strict because she's old.

GARNET: She was only cross when we were naughty.

RUBY: Never mind, we'll see her soon. (TWINS *snuggle for comfort. Pause.*)

GARNET: Perhaps we'd better go back.

RUBY: No, not yet. We have to stay away for ages and ages, and then Rose'll be really worried. Better to stay away until Dad gets back, then he'll be dead worried too, and they'll maybe have a go at each other. Then when we do turn up they'll be so relieved they won't go on at us. Or not so much anyway.

GARNET: Let's go back. Come on.

(TWINS *go home.* ROSE *is there wearing overall. She carries a can of red paint and paintbrush. Front door is now red.*)

GARNET: She's there!

(TWINS *turn to go but* ROSE *sees them.*)

ROSE: It's all right. I don't mind about the silly water – and no, I didn't tell your dad. Look. We've finished painting the shop. What do you think? (*Sees Garnet's dirty jeans.*) Blimey, Garnet, you're in a bit of a mess. I'll tell you what, give me your jeans later and I'll wash them through for you.

GARNET (*to* RUBY): She isn't even fussed. Gran would have gone mad.

RUBY: What's this? Love Rosy-Posy Day?

GARNET: No. I can't stick her, you know that, but . . .

(MRS LAVENHAM *enters.*)

MRS LAVENHAM: Red paint in the village high street? Disgusting!!

(MRS LAVENHAM *exits.* ROSE *blows raspberry after her. They all laugh.*)

ROSE: We'll show her. We'll show all of them . . . All right, girls – ready for your first day at school tomorrow? (ROSE *and* TWINS *exit.*)

(*Music in. Classroom.* SCHOOLCHILDREN *bring on easel and drawing boards. Offstage.* TWINS *change clothes.*)

BLOB: Oi, Ferret, how long have we gotta come in early for?

31

FERRET: Well, Miss Debenham says we've got to come in early until we learn to behave.

BLOB: Ahhh man, how long is that gonna take? And does Judy still have to sit between us?

FERRET: Yeah.

BLOB: Oh no, I can't stick her.

(TWINS *enter.*)

RUBY: It's awful, a little toy school, and as for the teacher . . .

(*Music in.* BLOB *and* FERRET *hold up the reverse side of three drawing boards that collectively make cut-out picture of gruesome teacher, with a hole where the face is.* MISS DEBENHAM *puts face through.* MISS DEBENHAM, BLOB *and* FERRET *make gruesome faces.*)

GARNET: Miss Debenham isn't a bit like that, Ruby.

(*Cut-out is removed to reveal real* MISS DEBENHAM.)

MISS DEBENHAM: Hello there, girls. Welcome to your new school. Now (*looking at* GARNET) your name is . . . ?

GARNET: Garnet.

(JUDY *enters at back.*)

MISS DEBENHAM (*looking at* RUBY): Right, so you must be Ruby. Attention please, boys and girls, we have two new pupils

starting today, Ruby and Garnet.
They've just moved here from the city
and I hope you'll make them both very
welcome. Now, would you two like to sit
together?

TWINS: Yes, please.

MISS DEBENHAM: Jolly good. How about over
there? Off you go. Oh, I've just got to get
the felt pens. Behave yourselves, everyone.
(*Exits.*)

BLOB: Ferret . . . (*Shows* FERRET *jar of
worms.*) Ha, ha, ha. (JUDY *sees them and
screams.* BLOB *takes out two worms then
creeps up to* TWINS.) Hello, girls, want
some friends to play with? (*Puts a worm
down each* TWIN's *neck.*)

GARNET: Ugh, it's a worm!

(GARNET *throws it away.* RUBY *yanks at
her worm, then holds it up.*)

RUBY: OK, Blob, you can take your stupid
little worm straight back.

(RUBY *sticks it down* BLOB's *trousers. He
doesn't like it.*)

JUDY: Jeremy Threadgold put a worm down
my neck once. I nearly went bananas.

(MISS DEBENHAM *enters with pot of felt
pens.*)

MISS DEBENHAM: Right, now, today we're
going to brighten up the classroom by

33

doing big pictures about Noah's ark. Do you know about Noah's ark, you two? (TWINS *nod*.) Jolly good. Now, class, you remember about Noah's ark? Yes you do, Jeremy – we did it last term, where the animals go in two by two. (BLOB *looks vague*.) Right, what animals shall we have? Brian . . . ?

FERRET: Lions, miss.

MISS DEBENHAM: Good boy, Brian – lions. Judy?

JUDY: Penguins, miss.

MISS DEBENHAM: Penguins – good. Monkeys – yes, that's a good one. Wombats . . . horses . . . Garnet?

GARNET: A giraffe!

MISS DEBENHAM: Good girl, Garnet. And you'll do a twin giraffe, right, Ruby?

RUBY: Wrong, Miss Debenham. I don't want to paint a silly giraffe. I'll do a flea.

GARNET: What? Why?

RUBY: Simple. One blob. Flea finished. Then I can just muck around for the rest of the lesson.

MISS DEBENHAM: So who'll do a giraffe with Garnet?

JUDY: I'll do a giraffe with Garnet, Miss Debenham.

MISS DEBENHAM: Good girl, Judy.

GARNET: No, I don't think—

MISS DEBENHAM: No, come on, Garnet, you said you'd like to do a giraffe, so you can do a giraffe with Judy. Never mind what Ruby wants to do. So let's get started. Choose your colours carefully.

(*All start pictures.* GARNET *and* JUDY *work at the easel.* RUBY *is jealous.* MISS DEBENHAM. *Walks around real or imaginary group.*)

MISS DEBENHAM: Wombats . . . What do they look like? Look it up in a book. Zebras? Like horses with stripes. Ah! Snakes, but snakes don't have legs. (*Sees easel.*) Oh, and what lovely giraffes. Well done, you two – gold stars! (*Moves on to* FERRET *and* BLOB.) Brian and Jeremy, very good . . . ?

BLOB: Man-eating sharks, miss.

MISS DEBENHAM: Yes, of course. Sharks. Now, Ruby, what an interesting flea. Is it going to have a friend? (*No response.*) I see.

(MISS DEBENHAM *moves on.* RUBY *moves over to* GARNET.)

RUBY (*hissing*): Lovely giraffes! Tell that stupid girl to go away.

GARNET: I can't. She's OK and she's good fun.

RUBY: Well, fine, you can be friends with her all you like. Just don't expect to be friends with me any more.

GARNET: Oh Ruby, please don't fight. You know I hate it when we fight. Ruby? (*School bell rings.*)

RUBY (*puts her hands over her ears*): Blah-blah-blah . . .

MISS DEBENHAM: Going home time, everyone. Come on, girls and boys. (*All exit school.*)

(TWINS *enter bedroom through door.*)

RUBY: Blah-blah-blah . . .

(RUBY *reads a* Beano *annual. Awkward silence.*)

GARNET: Look, I didn't mean to do things with Judy and leave you out. I'm really sorry.

(GARNET *puts arm around* RUBY *and then takes book away to get her attention.* RUBY *snatches book back and hits* GARNET *over the head with it.* GARNET *cries and moves downstage.* ROSE *enters and they bump into each other.*)

ROSE: Oh, sweetie, what is it? Don't cry. How was school? (*Silence.*) Look, I'm just about to pop out 'cos, guess what, there's a video shop down the road. There's nothing on telly tonight so I thought I'd get a film out. Why don't you come and help me choose one, eh? Come on, we'll get some chocolate too.

36

GARNET: I'd better not. I mean, I don't really feel like it.

ROSE: We could get *The Railway Children* — you love that, don't you? No? Oh Garnet, you don't always have to do what Ruby wants. Tell you what, go and see if she wants to come with us.

GARNET: She won't. I know. But thanks anyway.

> (ROSE *exits.* GARNET *moves upstage to twins' room. They are uneasy with each other. Then* GARNET *tickles* RUBY *and makes her laugh.*)

GARNET: Friends again?

RUBY: Yeah, OK, OK – get off me!

GARNET: Make friends, make friends, never, never break friends—

RUBY: With my twin sister and best friend Garnet Barker and not that stupid Judy person. Here, you can have some of my sweet.

GARNET: Ugh! It's all chewed and slobbery.

RUBY: So? We're twins, aren't we? Your slobber is the same as my slobber. My drool is the same as your drool. My spit is the same as your spit.

GARNET: Your spit is a lot *splashier* than mine.

RUBY: Let's prove it, tomorrow!

37

(*The next day. School yard.* SCHOOL-CHILDREN *appear.* BLOB *and* FERRET *pretend to play football.*)

BLOB: And here comes David Beckham.

FERRET: Hey, look at me, Alan Shearer.

JUDY: I'm playing here.

BLOB: No you're not. Move out the way . . . What shall we play?

FERRET: *Lord of the Rings.* I'll be an Orc.

(BLOB *and* FERRET *have a sword fight. They finish and spot* TWINS.)

BLOB: Ferret! Look. (*Moves over to between* TWINS.) Hello, twice as 'orribles. Twin townies. (TWINS *talk silently.*) What's the matter? (*More talk.*) What? (*More talk.*) I can't hear you.

TWINS: Then wash your ears out. (*Spit in* BLOB'S *ears.*)

BLOB: Ugh! Go on, Ferret, get her.

(TWINS, BLOB, FERRET *and* JUDY *start to fight.* MISS DEBENHAM *enters.*)

MISS DEBENHAM: Stop that at once! Did I see right? Ruby and Garnet spitting in Jeremy's ears! That's disgusting! You should be ashamed of yourselves. Into the classroom immediately – come along. (*All move to classroom.*) Garnet, go and get on with your giraffe.

GARNET: I'm doing a flea now, Miss Debenham.

MISS DEBENHAM: Oh, are you?
  (TWINS *put their hands up*.)
TWINS: Please may we go to the toilet, Miss
  Debenham?
MISS DEBENHAM: But you've just had break.
  You should have gone then instead of
  fighting. (TWINS *cross their legs*.) Oh, very
  well – off you go. (*Music in*.) Oh, dear. It
  looks like double trouble.
  (TWINS *do a twin walk off to music and
  bump into* JUDY, *ruining the giraffe
  picture*.)
JUDY: Oh no, my picture!
MISS DEBENHAM: Never mind, dear.
FERRET: Ha, ha, hard lines, Judy.
  (*All exit school, clearing easel and
  drawing boards*. TWINS *do mad-bad
  dance sequence. They enter living-room
  and are about to go to their room*. DAD
  *enters with two chairs and mobile
  phone. Another two chairs are brought
  on and put downstage*.)
DAD: No, come here, you two, and sit down.
  (TWINS *sit. On phone*) Yes, yes. I'm so
  sorry, Miss Debenham. Yes, I'll make sure
  they understand. Of course. Goodbye.
  (*Puts phone down*. ROSE *enters*.) Now, this
  is not good enough. That was your
  teacher, Miss Debenham. She says you're

not working at school and you never do as you're told. So why are you acting so stupidly?

ROSE: I think they act stupidly at home too!

RUBY (*to* ROSE): We only act —

GARNET: — stupid —

RUBY: — to stupid —

TWINS: — people.

(DAD *shakes them hard.* ROSE *sits at other side of stage.*)

DAD: Stop it! I won't have you talking to Rose like that. What's the matter with you? I just don't get it. You've always been such good girls. Well, you've had your moments, Ruby, but you've never behaved as badly as this before. You've always done well at school. I've been so proud of you. But now it seems as if you're going out of your way to be as naughty and disruptive as possible. You're not even trying to make friends with the other children. Miss Debenham says you've got into silly fights with the boys — and you upset one of the girls today. Judy someone? (RUBY *sniggers.* DAD *sighs.*) No. It's not funny. It's just unkind. I'm surprised at you both. (*To* GARNET, *who starts to cry*) Why do you always have to copy Ruby? You tried

really hard at first, but now you're
starting to be just as naughty as she is.
(*To* RUBY) Why can't you ever copy your
sister?

GARNET: I don't copy Ruby.

RUBY: I don't copy Garnet.

> (TWINS *copy each other, rubbing their
> eyes.* DAD *is unnerved.* ROSE *claps her
> hands.*)

ROSE: They ought to go on stage.

RUBY: Well ha, ha, ha, we're going to.

GARNET: Going to . . . (*Garnet is not so sure.*)

DAD: You're not going to go anywhere or be
anything unless you try harder at school.
So you'd better pull your socks up and get
started. Got it?

> (DAD *and* ROSE *exit.* GARNET *moves to
> side and picks up tray with dough,
> scissors, sellotape and newspaper on it.*)

RUBY: What you doing?

GARNET: Making dough twins.

RUBY: Can I make one?

> (GARNET *nods.* RUBY *starts to make one
> too.*)

RUBY: I'm going to give mine Doc Martens –
all the better for kicking with – ha, ha,
ha. No, I'm making Jeremy 'The Blob'
Threadgold . . . and now, I'm going to
torture him. (*Cuts up dough with*

41

blood-curdling noises. Spots newspaper.)
I know, I'm going to cut out some dolls.
(Starts to cut up paper.)

GARNET: No, stop it! That's Rose's *Guardian*.
She hasn't read it yet.

RUBY: Tough. *(Cuts, then pulls out dolls.
Starts to play, then stops, having spotted
something.)* Quick, where's the Sellotape?
(Finds it and sellotapes the paper.)

GARNET: Yes, Rose'll want to read that when
she gets back.

RUBY: Blow Rose. We've got to read it! Come
and take a look at this! Oh boy! No, oh
girl! Oh twin girl!

GARNET: Whatever are you burbling about?

RUBY: Look!

(Music in. GUARDIAN NEWSPAPER ADVERT
dances on. TWINS *turn to watch. Music
fades and held under the following.)*

GUARDIAN: Wanted: Girl twins. Sunnylea
Productions are going to turn Enid
Blyton's much-loved *Twins at St Clare's*
books into a children's television series.
Auditions start next Monday morning for
the plum parts, the twins themselves, so
any lively, outgoing twin girls with
showbiz ambitions can show up at
8 Newlake Street, London W1, at ten
o'clock, and be prepared to shine! *(Music*

up. Final dance from the ADVERT, *then to* TWINS) Yay! (Music out.)
(*Blackout. Music in to finish off act. Music out.*)

INTERVAL

ACT TWO

Living room.
> *(Music in. Lights up. Music fades.* TWINS
> *are in the same positions as at the end
> of act one.)*

RUBY: Wow! Lively, outgoing twins with
showbiz ambitions! This is it, Garnet!
Don't you see? Our chance of a lifetime!

GARNET: No.

RUBY: What?

GARNET: No. I can't.

RUBY: What do you mean? We can we can we
can. It's going to be difficult getting to
London by ten o'clock. We'll have to get up
ever so early. Rose will have to look after
the shop while Dad drives us. Still, that'll
be fun.

GARNET: No.

RUBY: Yes. Now, we're going to have to work
mega-fast preparing our audition piece. Go

45

and get book one quickly, and we'll learn one of the scenes.

GARNET: Ruby, I can't. I can't act for toffee — you know I can't.

RUBY: Look, it'll be fine. I promise you won't wet yourself this time.

GARNET: Stop it. It's not funny. I don't want to be in show business. You go if you want, but I'm not.

RUBY: Oh ha, ha, very helpful. How can I audition as a twin by myself, eh? Now, where's the book? We've got to get cracking. Which twin is which? I'll be the one that says the most. We'll work it so you don't have to say hardly anything, OK?

GARNET: No, Ruby, please, please.

RUBY: We can't miss out on this, Garnet. It's our big chance. We've got to go for it.

GARNET: But it says *lively*. I'm not a bit lively. I don't jump about like you. I just sort of flop in a corner. And I'm not outgoing. I'm as inward going as you could possibly get.

(DAD *and* ROSE *enter and freeze upstage.*)

RUBY: You'll be OK. Just copy me.

(TWINS *freeze downstage, then turn upstage as* DAD *and* ROSE *turn downstage.*)

DAD: Don't be daft. As if I'm going to drive you all the way to London at the crack of dawn on Monday! I don't want you and Garnet involved in any acting caper while you're still children. And I'm sorry, but I can't stick those simpering stage-school kiddiwinks. You're already enough of a show-off as it is.

ROSE: Oh, Rick, don't be so stuffy.

DAD: Stuffy?

ROSE: Yes. I don't see why they can't go to the audition. I reckon they'd walk away with the parts.

DAD: And just how are they going to get there?

ROSE: Well, I'll get up early on Monday and drive them. It's no big deal.

DAD: No way. There is no way I will allow them to go to that audition and that's that.

RUBY: But it's our lifetime ambition.

GARNET: *Your* ambition.

DAD: Ruby, I've said no and I mean no. Now there's an end to it. (*Exits.*)

ROSE: Sorry, girls. (*Follows* DAD.)

RUBY: After all we've done for him. Left Gran and all our friends to live in this horrible dusty old dump surrounded by mud and sheep with old Rosy rat-bag as our mother—

GARNET: *Step*mother. And she doesn't even want to be that. Just our friend. Anyway, there's no way you'll change Dad's mind. He won't take us.

RUBY: I know. But that's not going to stop us.

GARNET: What do you mean?

RUBY: What I say. I'll fix it. We'll just take ourselves.

(GARNET *exits*.)

(*Music in.* MR BAINES *enters and turns chair round to make videoshop. He sits and reads paper.* RUBY *enters. Music fades.*)

MR BAINES (*speaking loudly*): Hello, love. Want a video? Children's section's over there near Yoga and Keep Fit.

RUBY: Do you run a taxi firm?

MR BAINES: Yes, I do.

RUBY: Right, well, I'd like to order one for quarter past five next Monday morning to go to the station.

MR BAINES: A taxi? Whatever for? Why are you going to the station that early?

RUBY: Well, it's our gran's birthday and my dad, my sister and me are all going to London to celebrate.

MR BAINES: Oh, I see. Right then. Lovely. So it'll be your dad, you and the other one?

RUBY: Yes – my sister.

MR BAINES: Right, I'll just write that down. (*He writes on piece of paper.*) Three passengers, Monday morning at a quarter past five, OK? Well, if you're sure it's what you want. You *are* sure?

> (*Music in and out.* MR BAINES *exits with chair.*)

> (*Passage of time. Early Monday morning.* GARNET *enters, now in skirt and jacket. Inside house,* RUBY *changes clothes.*)

GARNET (*whispering*): Hurry up, we're late . . . It's all *your* fault. Why didn't you get up when I told you to?

RUBY (*off*): I've been up all night preparing everything. Where's my shoe?

GARNET: There – look under the bed.

RUBY: Right, thanks. Go and check if Mr Baines is there . . . I had to sell my silver locket and Gran's china doll, plus I took a few notes from the till—

GARNET: What!?

RUBY: We'll pay it back later. (*Enters in skirt with jacket and bag.*) Right, I'm ready, come on . . .

> (TWINS *move downstage. They are now outside. It is dark and cold.*)

GARNET: I can't believe we're really going.

RUBY: Oh, where is he? I hope we haven't missed him.

(MR BAINES *enters*.)

MR BAINES (*booms*): Morning.

RUBY: Sssh!!

MR BAINES: Sorry I'm a bit late. So, where's your dad?

RUBY: Um, he's got a tummy bug so he can't travel.

MR BAINES: Oh well, in that case—

RUBY: No, he's promised to send us on our own.

MR BAINES: What? Two young girls like you? All the way to London?

RUBY: Yes, we've got the money and Gran's going to meet us off the train. And we absolutely have to get there or she'll be heart-broken—

MR BAINES: Well, I'm not sure, not sure at all—

RUBY: Please, Mr Baines. Granny needs us. Please.

MR BAINES: No, I'm really not sure . . .

RUBY (*after a pause*): Oh well. We tried. Poor Gran. She'll be so disappointed . . .

MR BAINES (*after a pause*): Oh, come on, then. Hop in and let's get going. Seems odd to me, but then anything goes these days. (*Exits*.)

RUBY: Yippee! London, here we come!

(*Music in and sound effects collage.*
TWINS *move two of the chairs sideways
and sit as if on train.*)

TICKET INSPECTOR (*off stage*): Tickets, please!
(TICKET INSPECTOR *enters. He mimes
punching* TWINS' *tickets and looks
suspicious. Sound of train arriving at
station.* TWINS *get up and move.* BUSINESS-
WOMAN *enters and turns the chairs
sideways to create underground ticket
barrier. Others enter as travellers,
citizens, business people.* TWINS *watch,
then copy going through barrier. Group
assembles as on underground platform.
Sound effects of train arriving and
'Mind the gap!'. Group mime getting on
train, the journey and getting off.
Sound effects now of a busy London
street.* BUSINESSMAN *hails taxi,* TWINS
hail taxi. BUSINESSMAN *indicates it's
his.* TWINS *are bewildered and about to
panic. They try again and succeed. Sit
on chairs as if in taxi, then get out at
Newlake Street. Chairs cleared off by
passers-by. Sound effects of quiet
street.*)

RUBY: Trains, taxis – it's all so expensive, but
we've just enough. Look, we're here,
Newlake Street! Don't you dare cry,

Garnet, we don't want you all red-eyed
and bleary. Now come on. There's a sign.
We've got to go down this way.

(*Sound effects fade.* TWINS *exit.* MUM 1
*enters from opposite side with card-
board cut-out twins and forms a
queue.*)

MUM 1: Now, Sadie, Saffron, remember what
I told you. Breathe deeply, smile sweetly
and think to yourselves, 'I've got a
wonderful secret and all will be well.' Now
repeat after me, La la la, la, la, la.

(MUM 2 *enters and lines up behind*
MUM 1.)

MUM 2: Of course, Augusta, Jemima, of
course you'll get the parts, you're so
pretty. Oh look, here's the queue . . . Good
morning.

(TWINS *enter.*)

GARNET: Oh no! I've never seen so many
twins. We don't stand a hope. Let's go
home.

RUBY: We've come all this way and we're not
going back now. We're going to act better
than any of them.

GARNET: But I can't act at all.

RUBY: Look, those two are boys! They obviously
haven't read the book unless they're going
to put on frocks and wigs!

GARNET: But look at some of the others. I bet they've been to acting school.

RUBY: So? I've done my best to teach you. Now come on, let's go over our parts.

GARNET: Out here in front of everyone?

RUBY: We'll just do it in whispers, OK? We'll do the scene with the twins having a battle with Mam'zelle. I'll do Mam'zelle as well.

GARNET: What if we have to sing?

RUBY: We'll sing . . . er – not a pop song, they'll all do that. I know: we could do 'My Bonnie Lies Over the Ocean' with hand gestures.

GARNET: I'm not singing, especially not with hand gestures! And anyway, you know we can't sing in tune, either of us.

RUBY: Well, we could just sort of say the words, with lots of expression. And if we have to dance, well . . . we'll just have to jump around and jiggle a bit. Improvise. You copy me, OK? Us next. We're going to be great, Garnet. Better than any of this dopey stupid showy-offy lot. And it won't be scary, I promise. Trust me. Twin-grin.

GARNET (*unsure*): Twin-grin.

> (TWINS *exit. Lights down. Spotlight up.* CASTING TEAM *enter and move two chairs to sit in light.*)

CASTING AGENT: You know, Tarquin, I still think Letitia and Lulu have great potential.

CASTING ASSISTANT: You really think so?

AGENT: Yeah.

ASSISTANT: You see, I felt that their energy was sporadic. I would go with Becky and Joanna.

AGENT: Oh, I still don't know.

ASSISTANT: No?

AGENT: No. Next!

(TWINS *enter nervously*.)

AGENT: Hi, twins. Come on in.

RUBY: Hi.

AGENT: Hi. And you are?

RUBY: Ruby and Garnet Barker. We've got our audition piece all prepared. I'm Pat and she's Isabel and I'm also Mam'zelle as well, and then at the end I'm Janet as well.

AGENT: Well, we'd love to see your little number sometime, twins, but right now we just want to test your voices. Soooo . . . twin number one – to the camera please. If you could tell us what you had to eat yesterday.

RUBY: OK, well, breakfast was boring old muesli again. We used to have Coco Pops and they were yummy, but now we live with this awful woman, our dad's girlfriend, and she's into healthy foods, so it's hello, muesli. (DAD *arrives through the auditorium and watches*.) All this oat and bran. It makes your face ache munching and there's little raisins that look like rabbit droppings. Yuck!

AGENT: Very good. OK. And twin number two. Hi. To the camera, please, and if you could tell us what you had for lunch yesterday.

(GARNET *has seen* DAD *and cannot speak*.)

RUBY: Come on, Garnet . . . Look, I'll say what we had for lunch.

AGENT: It's all right, sweetie, we've already heard you. We want your twin to talk. OK, let's cut lunch and supper. What time did you go to bed, twin two?

GARNET (*mumbles*): Well, we start getting ready for bed at nine – ten at weekends – but we often try to stay up . . .

(GARNET *stops*. CASTING AGENT *shakes her head*.)

AGENT: Right. OK. Good. Thank you, twins – off you go. Next!

RUBY: No, wait! Look, my sister isn't very well. She can speak up and be ever so funny, I promise. If you'll just let us do a little bit from our audition piece? See, we've come all this way and we're going to get into terrible trouble—

AGENT: I know, sweetie, it's such a shame,
but we don't really have the time.

CASTING TEAM: Bye!

(TWINS *exit and take off jackets.*)

AGENT: Oh dear. You fancy a coffee?

ASSISTANT: Sophie, I could kill for one.

AGENT: It's such a shame – you know, that
kid was terrific.

ASSISTANT: Yeah, you can say that again. It's
a pity about the twin. (*This becomes an
echo, getting louder.*) Pity about the twin,
pity about the twin, pity about the twin,
twin, twin . . .

(CASTING AGENT *and* ASSISTANT *exit.* DAD
climbs onstage.)

(*Passing of time. Home.* DAD *enters.*
TWINS *enter, looking sheepish.*)

DAD: You bet you're in terrible trouble. How
dare you run off like that when I expressly
forbade it. I couldn't believe it when I
woke up and found you both gone. I was so
worried, I was going to call the police, but
Rose insisted you'd obviously gone for that
idiotic audition, so I had to go chasing
after you all the way to London—

RUBY: You're such a worry-guts. Whatever
could have happened to us on a simple
trip to London—?

DAD: Don't argue back!

RUBY: Well, it was a complete waste of time anyway. You really blew it for us, Dad. We were doing just great and then you had to come barging in and put us off our stroke—

DAD: What!!

(TWINS *sit*.)

GARNET: Put *me* off. Not you. And it wasn't Dad's fault. He waited. He gave us a chance. But I mucked it up. That's what they said. You were great, Ruby, yeah. But I was useless. They said so.

RUBY: No they didn't. And anyway, they didn't give you a proper chance. It wasn't fair.

DAD: You're not listening, are you? You really have no idea how dangerous it was going off like that or how much worry you've caused. And I don't care how important it seemed at the time. It was stupid, dangerous and very, very selfish. Got it? And anyway, you don't want to be an actress, Garnet. And even if you'd both been offered the parts, I wouldn't have let you take them, understand? Ruby can act when she grows up, but I don't want my girls turning into ghastly child stars, thank you very much.

(ROSE *enters. She and* DAD *sit opposite*
TWINS.)

GARNET (*to* RUBY): There's no chance of me
being any sort of star.

RUBY (*to* GARNET): Me neither. Now we're just
child nobodies stuck in this dreary dump
for ever and ever. And we've lost all our
savings.

DAD (*to* ROSE): Fancy not realizing how
dangerous it was, going all the way to
London on their own.

ROSE: I think they've learnt their lesson.

DAD: I felt like smacking them.

ROSE: You didn't, did you?

DAD: Of course not. I never have and I never
will.

RUBY (*to* GARNET): I wish he *would* smack us,
then we could show the bruises and be
taken into care.

ROSE: Well, I suppose it did show they were
ultra-determined and very clever—

DAD: Clever! Irresponsible and thoughtless,
more like. I just don't understand.

(DAD *moves upstage and takes off coat.*
Sound of TV permeates conversation.
Light flickers offstage.)

ROSE: Hey, look, look – quick, the telly.

DAD: What?

TV PRESENTER (*offstage*): Auditioning for the

new TV children's series, *The Twins at St Clare's* . . .

ROSE: The telly . . . Ruby, Garnet, quick – come and see the telly!

(TWINS *approach*.)

TV PRESENTER: London saw an extraordinary sight today. Hordes of twins descended upon the capital in the hope of being chosen. They came from all around Britain, full of expectation, but all but two have had their hopes dashed . . .

RUBY: It's us – yes, look, it's a close-up of me!

TV PRESENTER: This twin certainly took rejection like a trouper, and here are the winners . . .

RUBY: But look at who they've chosen. A pair of super-duper wallies!

TV PRESENTER: The film will be shot on location at Marnock Heights, a private girls' school with wonderful facilities, including a swimming pool, small zoo, playrooms with television, video, DVDs and its own theatre—

(DAD *turns off TV*.)

DAD: That's enough of that.

ROSE: Sounds exciting!

(TWINS *move away*.)

RUBY: Zoo, swimming pool, its own theatre! I

wish I could go to a school like that. Hey, wow, yes!

GARNET: No.

RUBY: Oh Garnet, come on. It would be absolutely fantastic. We'll write a letter applying.

GARNET: But I don't want to.

RUBY: Well I do. I really really really do. Anything to get away from here. (*Snaps her fingers.* POSTMAN *enters on a scooter.*) And it would be ultra-mean of you to muck up my chances again. Right? (*Writes a letter on* POSTMAN's *back.*) 'Dear Madam, We are twins and we hate our school in this village. We don't fit in and there aren't any proper books and the only games we play are rounders. When we saw your school on the TV we thought, Ohh, this is our idea of heaven. So please let us come to your school in September. We promise to be good pupils and you don't have to worry about us being homesick because we hate our home. Yours faithfully, Ruby and Garnet Barker . . . (*Music in.*) P.S. Please say yes. You won't regret it – honestly.'

(POSTMAN *scoots off. Everyone moves around and changes position.* POSTMAN *re-enters and gives them reply letter, then exits.* TWINS *take letter to* DAD. *Music fades.*)

DAD: (*opens letter*): What's all this about?

RUBY: We're not kidding, Dad. We read all the *St Clare's* books when we were waiting to act in the telly series. And we think it all sounds really great. So Garnet and I want to go to boarding school.

DAD: But it's not like it is in the books. I don't think either of you would go a bundle on a real boarding school. For instance, you have to work hard and do as you're told. According to Miss Debenham, you don't do any work at all and never do as you're told.

RUBY: Yes, but that's because she's a silly teacher and it's a silly school.

DAD: Don't be so rude—

RUBY: But if we went to a super top-notch boarding school then we'd be mega-good, all the time. A boarding school like Marnock Heights.

DAD: Like *where*?

RUBY: It's the place they're using for the *St Clare's* film. It's a real school. So Garnet and I wrote to the headmistress asking to go there and she's sent us this brochure all about it – look! (*Indicates brochure.*)

DAD: Oh, for goodness' sake! Will you girls *stop* doing things behind my back.

RUBY: Say we can go, though, Dad, *please*. Look at all the pictures. It's lovely, isn't it?

DAD: Oh, very lovely. And very lovely school fees too! Eight thousand pounds a year. Each! Oh yes, nice one, Ruby.

RUBY: Oh no!

GARNET: Oh no.

RUBY: I didn't realize you had to pay.

ROSE: Wait a minute – Look, there's a letter. (*Reading*) 'Dear Ruby and Garnet, What lovely names! You wrote me a lovely letter too. I'm pleased that you'd like to attend Marnock Heights. Here is the current prospectus. Show it to your parents or guardians. I'd like to point out that we do award several special scholarships each year. One girl is now unable to take up her scholarship because she's going abroad. Perhaps you'd like to sit the examination to see if either of you might pass highly enough for scholarship consideration? Please tele-phone my secretary for an appointment. With best wishes, yours sincerely, Miss Jeffreys, Headteacher.'

RUBY: Wow!

DAD: No.

RUBY: But—

DAD: I said no!

ROSE: Well, I think they should go for it. It's a wonderful opportunity.

DAD: But—

ROSE: Honestly, Rick, it's a great chance. It's ever such a famous school. If one of them got a scholarship there then they'd be able to go on, do anything, achieve anything. They were really disappointed about the audition, so let them try for this, please?

DAD: Well . . .

RUBY: Yippee!

(DAD *and* ROSE *exit.*)

(TWINS *take a chair each and sit. Passage of time. Exams in school. Clock ticks.* TEACHER *paces.* TWINS *are in spotlights. They mime writing.*)

TEACHER: Please listen carefully. The subject for your composition is 'Snow in Winter'. Pick up your pens. You have twenty minutes, starting now.

(GARNET *smiles.* RUBY *grimaces. We hear a voice-over collage of what they are writing.*)

RUBY: '. . . In winter it is jolly. People hang up holly and robins hop about . . .'

63

GARNET: '. . . Once, when we were making snow angels in the park, I stopped moving my arms and legs to see what it would be like to be frozen . . .'

RUBY: '. . . And icicles go drip, drip on your head . . .'

GARNET: '. . . And the snow looks so clean and pure, but nothing's dirtier when everyone's trudged through it and it's all grey with yellow patches . . .'

RUBY: '. . . And we go crunch, crunch on the snow . . .'

GARNET: '. . . It's always like that. It can't ever stay the same . . .'

RUBY: '. . . And the jolly robin goes hop, hop all over the place. The end.'

GARNET: '. . . And yet each time you hope there'll be a way of keeping it looking beautiful.'

TEACHER: Time's up. Finish writing please and put down your pens.

> (*Music in.* TEACHER *collects imaginary papers and exits. Chairs are moved to former position. Home.* POSTMAN *enters with letter.* DAD *opens it.* POSTMAN *exits. Music fades.* DAD *and* ROSE *face the* TWINS. *There's a stunned silence.*)

RUBY: She means me. She must mean me.

GARNET: Yes, it can't be me. Ruby will have got the scholarship.

DAD: No, it's definitely Garnet.

RUBY: Let me see the letter!

DAD: It's addressed to me. And it's plain what it says. There's no mix-up.

RUBY: Miss Jeffreys just got our names round the wrong way. It's always happening.

ROSE: Not this time.

RUBY: Look, it's not fair if she's read the letter and I haven't, when it's got nothing to do with her. She's not our mother.

DAD: No, but I'm your father, and I want you to calm down, Ruby, and we'll talk all this over carefully.

RUBY: Not till you show me the letter!

ROSE: Show them, Rick. They're not little kids. I think they should see what it says.

(DAD *shows them the letter, which* GARNET *scans.*)

GARNET (*reading*): 'Ruby is charming and a natural actress but failed several of our tests . . . I feel she's relied on her sister to do all her work . . . Garnet too might benefit from a term of separation from her sister . . . few gaps in knowledge . . . but on the whole did extremely well . . . essay outstanding . . . sensitive and mature . . . We would like to offer her a full scholarship, commencing in the autumn term . . . Miss Jeffreys, Headteacher.' She's written a whole load of rubbish. She only met us for one afternoon and yet she thinks she knows us. Well, she doesn't, does she? Ruby? Oh look, I'm not even going to Marnock Heights. I didn't want to go in the first place. It was you that wanted to, not me.

ROSE: Well, I think you should go. You've done very well. We should all be busy congratulating you. I know it's tough on Ruby, but—

GARNET (*shouts*): You don't know anything.

DAD: Hey, we'll have less of that cheeky tone. Rose, love, could you make us all a cup of coffee? Let's talk it over, eh? It's been a bit of a shock for all of us. (ROSE *exits*. RUBY *starts to exit*.) Ruby? Ruby, where are you going?

RUBY: There's nothing to talk about. Garnet's got the scholarship. I haven't. And that's that.

GARNET: But I'm not going! Please believe me. I couldn't stand going there. Especially without you. (*Makes* RUBY *sit down*.)

RUBY: So why did you try ever so hard in all those silly tests and write all that yucky stuff for your essay?

GARNET: I don't know. I just didn't think. I'm sorry. (*Tries to hug* RUBY.)

RUBY: Get away from me. (*Starts to exit.* DAD *stops her.*)

DAD: Now this is getting ridiculous. Pull yourself together, Ruby. I'm ashamed of you. Why can't you be big enough to congratulate your sister? She didn't act like this over that television audition, now did she? She was full of praise for you.

RUBY (*about to cry*): Oh, congratulations, clever goody-goody Garnet.

(RUBY *exits.* GARNET *starts to follow her.* DAD *stops her.*)

DAD: No. Let her go. She won't want you around for a bit, especially as she's crying. But there's no need for you to cry, sweetheart. Rose is right. You've done brilliantly and I'm very proud of you.

GARNET (*cries*): I'm not going though.

(GARNET *sits.* DAD *sits next to her.* ROSE *enters with coffee.*)

DAD: Well. I can't *make* you go. And this boarding-school lark certainly wasn't my idea. But I do think now that it's a wonderful opportunity.

ROSE: I'll say. (*Hands out coffee.*) You've got to go for it, Garnet. You've done so well.

GARNET: But I can't leave Ruby.

ROSE: Ruby would leave you.

GARNET: That's different.

DAD: But it shouldn't be different. (ROSE *exits*.) This letter's made me see that maybe it's bad for you two to be together all the time. You're holding each other back, spoiling each other's chances. You're growing up and you need to develop as separate sisters.

GARNET: But we're not separate. We're twins. We can't do without each other.

DAD: You're going to have to learn to some day. You'll both grow up and have different jobs and have different lifestyles and have different families—

GARNET: No, we're going to stay together always – we've got it all worked out. We're going to marry twins and have twin babies and then when they grow up they'll stick together and maybe they'll have twins and then they could . . . and they could . . .

(GARNET *moves upstage in distress.* DAD *exits with coffee cups.*)

GARNET: Ruby! (RUBY *enters.* GARNET *sees* RUBY *has scissors. She has cut her plaits off and now has short, scruffy hair and is wearing jeans.*) What have you done?

RUBY: I'm making me different. And you needn't look like that. I like it. I wanted it this way for ages – sort of punk. Great. (GARNET *grabs scissors.*) No, don't you dare. (*Snatches scissors back.*) I'm warning you – you cut off your hair and I'll cut off your head! (*Throws down the scissors and turns away.*)

GARNET: Could we go back to being us if I wrote a letter to Miss Jeffreys saying I wasn't going to Marnock Heights?

RUBY: It doesn't matter what you do. We're not us any more and we won't ever be again. We'll still be split up even if we stay together. You do what you like. And I'll do what I like.

GARNET: But it's not what I like.

RUBY: Tough!

(*Music in. Dance sequence as* GARNET *follows* RUBY, *who rejects her.* GARNET *collects scissors and exits.*)

RUBY: Ruby Barker doesn't give two hoots about not getting that stupid scholarship. Ruby Barker doesn't give two hoots about her sneaky sister getting it instead of her. Ruby Barker doesn't give two hoots about her sneaky sister.

(*Music swells and fades. Passage of time. Enter* ROSE *with carrier bag with new trainers.*)

ROSE: There you are. Your gran's just rung. She's coming for tea today with Mr Lewis so I've ironed all your best clothes and put them out for you upstairs. Please hurry up and get changed—

RUBY: No.

ROSE: But she'll go mad if she sees you like that. Please, for your dad's sake, if not for mine, make an effort?

RUBY: I'm staying as I am.

ROSE: Well, at least let me try and neaten up your hair. (RUBY *moves away*.) Oh, and look, I nipped out and got you some new trainers, so you can throw those old things in the bin. OK? (*Puts trainers on the floor*.)

RUBY: No, you can put *those* in the bin (*kicks trainers*), you can put your comb in the bin and you can put yourself in the bin. Just leave me alone!!

    (RUBY *exits*. ROSE *sighs, then pulls herself together and picks up trainers. Enter* DAD *with table*.)

DAD: They're here. Everything OK?

    (DAD *starts to add chairs*. GARNET *enters*.)

ROSE: I suppose so.

DAD: Good. Garnet, can you pop upstairs and get your sister please?

(GARNET *exits*. DAD *opens door to greet*
GRAN *and* MR LEWIS, *who have come for
tea. They both look very smart.* MR LEWIS
sports a button-hole.)

DAD: Hello, Gran, how nice to see you – you
look wonderful. Do come in.

GRAN: Thank you, Richard. Hello, Rose.

ROSE: Gran. And you, Mr Lewis. Welcome.
Please make yourselves at home. (*Exits.*)

MR LEWIS: Thanks, love.

GRAN: So where are the girls? Girls! We're
here. Come and meet your Uncle Albert.
(GARNET *enters.*) Garnet, my love, there
you are. (*Kisses* GARNET.)

MR LEWIS: Hello, Garnet.

(GARNET *shakes* MR LEWIS's *hand.* RUBY
enters.)

GRAN: Ruby? What*ever* have you done to yourself, Ruby? What *do* you look like? You're
such a scruff. Like a gutter child. And your
hair! Oh my lord, have you got nits?

RUBY: Leave off, Gran.

(ROSE *brings on teatray and cake.*)

ROSE: Let's all sit down.

DAD: Here, let me take your arm, Gran.
(*All sit.*)

GRAN: But for goodness' sake, Rose, how
could you let her run round like that, like
a – a ragamuffin?

ROSE: Ruby likes to be comfy. And we think her hairstyle really suits her, don't we, Ricky?

DAD: Sure.

ROSE: Mr Lewis – er, Uncle Albert, do have some cake.

MR LEWIS: Thank you, love.

(ROSE *hands* MR LEWIS *a pop-up slice of cake.*)

GRAN: Well, I've never seen anything like it. A granddaughter of mine looking like a guttersnipe. They were always well dressed when I looked after them. And dressed the same, like twins should be.

DAD: Have some cake.

GRAN: At least Garnet looks fairly present-able. But what's all this I hear about you being packed off to boarding school? I don't hold with that idea at all. Do you, Albert?

MR LEWIS: Well, I don't know really—

GRAN: What's the matter, do they want to get rid of you?

DAD: Of course we don't want to get rid of her! We just think she should give it a try for a term, seeing as she's won this scholarship. But if she hates it, then of course she can come home, whenever she wants.

GRAN: Oh. And I suppose that's all right then, is it?
    (*Pause.*)
MR LEWIS: Nice cake.
GRAN: Well, she doesn't look very happy to me. Are you happy, Garnet? And as for the other one, she just looks . . . barmy!
    (*Music in.* DAD, ROSE, GRAN *and* MR LEWIS *exit. Outside.* RUBY *wanders around for a while, followed by* GARNET.)
RUBY: Leave me alone. Stop following me. I said, *leave me alone!*
    (GARNET *exits.* GANG *appears and taunts* RUBY. BLOB *has black plastic bag of grass cuttings.*)
FERRET: Look at that. Are you sure it's a girl, Jerry?
BLOB: Nah, man.
FERRET: She's a freak!
GANG: Let's get her!
BLOB: Hey, Baldie! 'Ere, look – grass cuttings. Do you want a green wig?
    (BLOB *throws grass over* RUBY. *She grabs black rubbish bag from offstage.*)
RUBY: Ha, ha, very funny. All you lot do is talk a load of rubbish—
BLOB: Oh yeah?
RUBY: – so why don't you wear some? (*Tips contents over* GANG.)

73

BLOB: Get her, man, go on!
(*They fight.*)

WARREN: Go on, Jerry, bash her face in!

BLOB: Hey, let go of her, Ferret, she's
choking—

JASON: Well, hit her then!

BLOB: Not with him hanging onto her. And
all you others. Leave go of her. It's not
fair. We'll fight it out, just her and me. (*To*
RUBY) Are you all right?

RUBY: Yeah, course I am.

BLOB: Right. Let's fight.

(*Music in.* BLOB *pushes* RUBY, *who
pushes him back.* GANG *start to chant
'Fight, fight, fight.'* BLOB *lunges at* RUBY
*and they perform a series of carefully
choreographed grapples and lunges.
Then they fight in slow motion, with
exaggerated swings at each other and
contorted faces. This is to give the
impression of passing time.* GANG *also
moves in slow motion. The action reverts
to normal. The two fighters fall over
each other and roll on the ground.* GANG
members exit, bored. FERRET *stays. The
fighting stops and both examine their
injuries.*)

BLOB: Shall we just call it quits and say I
won?

RUBY: You haven't won the rotten fight!

BLOB: Shall we just call it a draw then?

RUBY: All right. But I *could* have won.

BLOB: You're quite a good fighter. For a girl.

RUBY: You're quite a good fighter. For a blob.

BLOB: Hey! You can stop calling me names. I saved you – I stopped Ferret-Face from mangling your neck.

RUBY: Yeah, but you called me names. Baldie.

BLOB: So? You do look a bit bald since you had that freaky haircut.

RUBY: So? You do look a bit blobby.

BLOB: So? At least were both good at fighting.

RUBY: Better than that Ferret-Face.

FERRET: Hey!

BLOB: You can say that again.

FERRET: Jerry!

BLOB: So where's your sister?

RUBY: Don't play with her any more. I haven't played with her all summer.

BLOB: Why not?

RUBY: I'm different.

(*Pause.*)

BLOB: Do you . . . do you want to be in our gang?

RUBY: OK.

BLOB: Come on then, Baldie.

RUBY: Keep your hair on, Blob.

(*Wild music in.* BLOB *leads* FERRET *and*

RUBY *in a short, wild dance, punching the air and shouting, full of exuberance and aggression but also quite funny.* BLOB *and* FERRET *then exchange the gang handshake and exit.* RUBY *carries on without them, slowing down when she realizes they've left her. Music fades. She is on her own.*)

RUBY: My sister can't manage without me but I'm doing fine without her. She's off to boarding school tomorrow. She's started crying at nights. She's scared. She says she can't bear not being friends with me any more. (*Slows right down.*) But I don't need her. Not one little bit of her. (*Curls up downstage and rocks herself.*) It feels like I'm snapping in half. Oh, Garnet . . .

(*The morning of Garnet's departure. Her trunk is pulled on by* ROSE. GARNET *enters in her new school uniform.*)

ROSE: There. Everything's ready. All your new things safely packed.

GARNET: Thanks for helping me with all this, Rose, and for making my favourite meal last night. I can't believe I'm going . . . I feel a bit sick.

ROSE: You'll be fine.

GARNET: But I'm so scared . . . Sorry, I need the loo.

(GARNET *exits.* RUBY *sits up and looks distraught.* ROSE *turns and sees her.*)

ROSE: I can't believe she's really going either. She's so nervous, poor thing. We're going to miss her so much. (*Whispers*) You're the one that never cries. You'll start me off.

RUBY: Don't be nice to me. I've been so hateful to Garnet.

ROSE: You haven't exactly been sweetness and light to me, either. Or your dad. But you're right. It's Garnet that matters. Especially now.

(ROSE *exits as* GARNET *enters. She sees* RUBY *and is about to exit but* RUBY *stops her.*)

RUBY: Oh, Garnet, I'm so sorry. I've been such a mean pig. I didn't mean it really. I was just jealous, and I felt stupid and left out. You will still be my twin, won't you, even though you're off to boarding school?

GARNET: Of course. I'll be your twin for ever and ever and ever.

RUBY: I'll miss you so much.

GARNET: I'll miss you too – ever so ever so much. But Dad says if I really hate it, I can come back whenever I want.

RUBY: And you'll come home some weekends – and all the holidays . . . Why do I always have to be the bad twin? (*Moves and sits downstage.* GARNET *joins her.*)

GARNET: Why do I always have to be the good twin? Hey, maybe we're changing round. We're starting already. You're crying – and I'm not!

RUBY: You will still be my best friend, won't you? You won't go all posh and snooty?

GARNET: Don't be daft.

RUBY: And you will write?

GARNET: Every single day. And you write to me too.

RUBY: I promise.

GARNET: You don't always keep your promises.

RUBY: But I'll keep this one, I swear. And I also promise I'll never be mean to you ever again.

GARNET: Oh Ruby!

(GARNET *laughs. They hold hands.* DAD *enters.*)

DAD: Come on, time to go. (TWINS *stand.*) I'm really glad you two have made it up. I'm so proud of you both. (*Hugs them. To* RUBY) Keep your chin up, my little Scrubbing Brush. I'll be back soon. Bye, Rose. (*Exits with trunk.*)

GARNET: Thanks, Rose. (*Kisses* ROSE.)

ROSE: Now you take care.

(GARNET *and* RUBY *give twin handshake,
then hug, not wanting to let go.* GARNET
*breaks away and heads for door,
followed by* ROSE.)

GARNET: See ya.

ROSE: Bye.

(GARNET *exits. Sound effects of car
driving off.*)

ROSE: There she goes. (*Pause.* ROSE *closes
door then moves downstage.*) By the way,
Ruby, I meant to tell you – I discovered
there's a drama club in Hineford on
Saturdays. It sounds really good. They do
their own plays and seem to have a great
time. I was wondering if you'd like to join?
I can drive you there.

RUBY: Thanks, Rose.

ROSE: It's OK. I'm dying to go to town to get
to some decent shops. I tell you what, you
could do your drama club, then we could
meet up and have lunch. Yes?

RUBY: You're on. Thanks. (*Crosses to* ROSE
and hugs her for the first time. ROSE *holds
her tight.*)

ROSE (*whispers*): It'll be all right. You'll see.

(ROSE *exits.* RUBY *collects letter from
offstage then moves into spot downstage.*

GARNET *appears in spotlight downstage on other side.* GARNET *speaks as* RUBY *reads letter.*)

GARNET: 'Dearest Ruby (*Music in*). I'm here, at Marnock Heights! I feel just like one of the girls in those old school books. I cried a bit after Dad left but this lovely girl called Jamila cheered me up. She's going to look after me. I'm in the bedroom now and there are three other girls and we're all setting our alarms for midnight so we can have our first feast! The girl in the bed next to me is called Lucy, and she wears glasses. She's got a rabbit in the zoo and she says I can share it if I want. She wants to be my best friend and I said yes, but you're my *bestest* best friend. With lots and lots of love, from Garnet. P.S. I do miss you so.'

RUBY: Oh, Garnet. I miss you too. Ever so ever so much. But we're still Ruby and Garnet, even though you're there and I'm here. We're going to be Ruby and Garnet for ever.

(*Music fades with lights. Lights up. Music in for curtain call.* TWINS *meet centre stage and hold hands. The rest join. Finale dance. Others exit.* TWINS *make final exit.*)

THE END

ABOUT THE AUTHOR

JACQUELINE WILSON was born in Bath in 1945, but has spent most of her life in Kingston-on-Thames, Surrey. She always wanted to be a writer and wrote her first 'novel' when she was nine, filling countless Woolworths' exercise books as she grew up. She started work at a publishing company and then went on to work as a journalist on *Jackie* magazine (which was named after her) before turning to writing fiction full-time.

Since 1990 Jacqueline has written prolifically for children and has won many of the UK's top awards for children's books, including the Guardian Children's Fiction Award, the Smarties Prize and the Children's Book of the Year. Jacqueline was awarded an OBE in the Queen's Birthday Honours list, in Goldeen Jubilee Year, 2002.

Over 15 million copies of Jacqueline's books have now been sold in the UK and approximately 50,000 copies of her books are sold each month. An avid reader herself, Jacqueline has a personal collection of more than 15,000 books.

She has one grown-up daughter.

THE DIAMOND GIRLS

Jacqueline Wilson

'You're all my favourite Diamond girls,' said Mum.
'Little sparkling gems, the lot of you . . .'

Dixie, Rochelle, Jude and Martine – the Diamond girls!
They might sound like a girl band but these sisters' lives
are anything but glamorous. They've moved into a
terrible house on a run-down estate and after barely five
minutes Rochelle's flirting, Jude's fighting and Martine's
storming off. Even though Dixie's the youngest, she's
desperate to get the house fixed up before Mum comes
home – with her new baby! Will the Diamond girls pull
together in time for the first Diamond boy?

A typical slice of real life – tough on the outside,
warm on the inside – from the bestselling,
multi-award-winning Jacqueline Wilson.

Now available in Doubleday hardcover

0 385 60607 9

BEST FRIENDS

Jacqueline Wilson

*Alice is my very best friend. I don't
know what I'd do without her.*

Gemma and Alice have been best friends since they
were born. They see each other every day. It never
seems to matter that Gemma loves football while Alice
prefers drawing or that Gemma never stops talking
while Alice is more likely to be listening. They share
everything. Then one day Gemma finds out that
there's something Alice isn't sharing. A Secret. And
when Gemma finally discovers what it is, she isn't
sure if she and Alice can stay Best Friends Forever . . .

A delightfully touching and entertaining story
from a best-selling, prize-winning author.

Now available in Doubleday hardcover

0 385 60606 0

THE ILLUSTRATED MUM

Jacqueline Wilson

*Star used to love Marigold, love me, love our life
together. We three were the colourful ones,
like the glowing pictures inked all over Marigold . . .*

Covered from head to foot with glorious tattoos,
Marigold is the brightest, most beautiful mother in
the world. That's what Dolphin thinks (she just
wishes her beautiful mum wouldn't stay out partying
all night or go weird now and then). Her older sister,
Star, isn't so sure any more. She loves Marigold too,
but sometimes she just can't help wishing she
were more normal . . .

A powerful and memorable tale for older readers
from Jacqueline Wilson, the award-winning
author of *The Suitcase Kid*, *Double Act*,
Bad Girls and many other titles.

WINNER OF THE 2000 BRITISH BOOK AWARD (NIBBIES)
WINNER OF THE CHILDREN'S BOOK OF THE YEAR AWARD
WINNER OF THE GUARDIAN CHILDREN'S FICTION AWARD
HIGHLY COMMENDED FOR THE CARNEGIE MEDAL

Corgi Yearling Books

0 440 86368 6

BAD GIRLS
Jacqueline Wilson

*Kim's gang had better watch out! Because Tanya's
my friend now, and she'll show them*

Mandy has been picked on at school for as long as she
can remember. That's why she is delighted when
cheeky, daring, full-of-fun Tanya picks her as a friend.
Mum isn't happy – she thinks Tanya's a BAD GIRL
and a bad influence. Mandy's sure Tanya can only get
her out of trouble, not in to it . . . or could she?

SHORTLISTED FOR THE CARNEGIE MEDAL

Corgi Yearling Books

0 440 86356 2

For all the latest news, information
and events and to join the official
Jacqueline Wilson Fan Club,
log on to

www.jacquelinewilson.co.uk